Scottish Fold Cats

BY TAMMY GAGNE

The Child's World

Published by The Child's World®
1980 Lookout Drive • Mankato, MN 56003-1705
800-599-READ • www.childsworld.com

Acknowledgments
The Child's World®: Mary Berendes, Publishing Director
Red Line Editorial: Editorial direction
The Design Lab: Design
Amnet: Production
Design elements: Onishchenko Natalya/Shutterstock Images;
iStockphoto; Shutterstock Images; Africa Studio/Shutterstock
Images; Willem Havenaar/Shutterstock Images

Photographs ©: Onishchenko Natalya/Shutterstock Images,
cover, 1, 23; iStockphoto, cover, 1, 13, 17; Shutterstock Images,
cover, 1, 15, 19, 20; Africa Studio/Shutterstock Images, cover, 1;
Willem Havenaar/Shutterstock Images, cover, 1; Loginova Elena/
Shutterstock Images, 5; Mitchell Kranz/Shutterstock Images, 6;
Mikhail Valeev/Shutterstock Images, 9; Nikita Starichenko/
Shutterstock Images, 11

ISBN 9781626873865
LCCN 2014930642

Printed in the United States of America
Mankato, MN
July, 2014
PA02226

ABOUT THE AUTHOR

Tammy Gagne has written dozens of books about the health and behavior of animals for both adults and children. Her most recent titles include Great Predators: Crocodiles *and* Super Smart Animals: Dolphins. *She lives in northern New England with her husband, son, and a menagerie of pets.*

CONTENTS

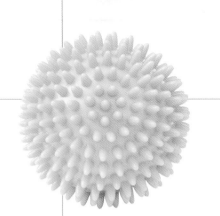

Great Scot!

Some people think Scottish fold cats look like teddy bears. Other people are reminded of an owl when they see these cats. This special **breed** is eye-catching. Scottish folds have round heads with ears that fold forward. This gives them their special look.

Not only does this breed have a special look, but they are also well behaved. Scottish folds are very social cats. They like spending time around people. They especially enjoy being with their owners.

Scottish folds do well with children. They also do well with other cats. They even like dogs! This makes Scottish folds a great family pet.

A Scottish fold's ears fall forward because a **gene** affects the **cartilage**.

Scottish fold cats' ears are what give these cats their name.

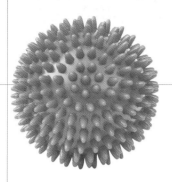

Not Like the Others

The Scottish fold is a newer cat breed. It was discovered in Scotland in 1961. A shepherd named William Ross came upon a barn cat. He noticed she looked different from other cats. Her ears folded forward.

This cat's name was Susie. She had a long white coat. Susie's mother had **upright** ears. No one knew what Susie's father looked like. He may have had folded ears, too. Or Susie may have been the first cat with special ears.

People liked how Susie looked. She was bred with other breeds. These included American shorthair, Burmese, and Persian cats. Susie's kittens also had folded ears. William Ross became the owner of one of these kittens. He named her Snooks.

Ross bred Snooks when she was old enough. But not all of the kittens had folded ears. Some had normal ears. A special gene produced the fold. But there was no way to tell which kittens would get it.

All true Scottish fold cats can be traced back to Susie.

Breeders do not know ahead of time if Scottish fold kittens will have folds in their ears.

An American Success Story

The Scottish fold breed arrived in the United States in 1970. A **geneticist** from Massachusetts bought three of Snooks' kittens. He wanted to study the kittens' genes. He hoped to learn more about what caused the folded ears.

The scientist did not continue his study for very long. He found homes for all three cats. One cat went to Salle Wolfe Peters in Pennsylvania. She began to breed her Scottish fold cat. This was the first Scottish fold to be bred in the United States. Peters wanted to have the breed added to the cat registry. This was not an easy task. But Peters worked hard to make it happen.

The Cat Fanciers' Association accepted the Scottish fold as an official breed in 1973. It soon became one of the ten most popular cat breeds in the United States.

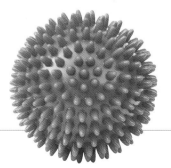

After arriving in the United States, Scottish folds quickly gained popularity for their looks and personality.

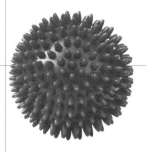

How Low Do They Go?

All Scottish fold litters include kittens with both ear types. But it takes a while to tell them apart. When they are about three weeks old, some of the kittens' ears begin folding forward.

A cat may end up with a single fold, a double fold, or a triple fold. A single fold bends forward at the midpoint of the ear. A double fold is tighter, bending lower. A triple fold lies nearly flat to the head. Cats with triple folds make the best show cats.

Scottish folds with straight ears are still members of the breed. These cats are not shown in cat shows. But they make great pets. They also tend to be less expensive than cats with folded ears.

Straight-eared Scottish folds are also used for breeding. At least one of the Scottish folds in a breeding pair should have folded ears. If both have this feature, the kittens' skulls can end up **misshapen**.

> About one half of Scottish fold kittens end up having folded ears.

All Scottish fold kittens are born with straight ears.
Their ears may begin to bend after about three weeks.

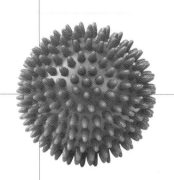

Sit Right Back

Scottish folds come in many colors and coat patterns. They may be one solid color or two colors. Some Scottish folds have a tabby coat.

Most of these cats have copper-colored eyes. But all common eye colors can also be found in the breed.

Scottish folds have either long or short hair. Susie, the first Scottish fold, had a long coat. Longhaired members of the breed were not officially recognized until the mid-1980s.

The Scottish fold is also known for its round shape. Its round face, eyes, and body give the cat a very sweet look. Even the nose looks curved when viewed from the side. The round body gives this medium-sized cat a chubby look. Scottish folds look especially round when they sit in their favorite position. It is called the Buddha pose. They sit back with their paws on their bellies. It is funny to see!

Scottish folds are loved for their special round shape.

Man's Other Best Friend

Scottish folds have sweet personalities. They usually bond with one special person in a household. Scottish folds will follow their favorite person around. It is similar to what dogs do with their owners.

Scottish folds get along with everyone, including other pets. Many cat breeds prefer to blend into the background. But the Scottish fold is anything but shy. It enjoys being in the center of the action.

Scottish folds also have curious personalities. They will often sit upright like prairie dogs to look around if they hear a noise.

This breed is also like a dog in how it plays. Owners can teach a Scottish fold to play games such as fetch. Scottish folds even enjoy water. Many of these cats will sit and play with running water.

Scottish folds can live in louder homes with kids. But they are also happy to spend quiet time.

Famous pop singer Taylor Swift owns a Scottish fold cat named Meredith. She likes to share funny pictures of her cat with fans.

Kittens remain playful as they move into adulthood. This breed loves attention. But they are not needy animals. They want to be near people, not on them.

Scottish folds enjoy attention from their owners, or toys to play with.

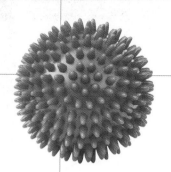

Follow the Leader

Owners of Scottish folds rarely go anywhere alone. These loving pets want to be where their owners are.

Some owners take their Scottish folds on vacation with them. This breed makes a good traveling buddy. Unlike many other breeds, it quickly gets used to new settings.

At home, Scottish folds enjoy company. If you are having a party, do not put this cat in another room. It will want to greet the guests as they arrive.

The breed is happy to spend time with kids or adults. If the party includes games, the Scottish fold will definitely want to play. These cats are true party animals.

But don't expect help cleaning up after the event. Your Scottish fold will use up all its energy being social. While you wash dishes, your pet will look for a nearby spot for a nap.

Scottish folds enjoy napping on their backs. This is one of the breed's favorite sleeping positions.

After a full day of playing, a Scottish fold will need a catnap.

Play Time!

Scottish folds are very smart. They are very good at figuring out puzzle toys. But their favorite games involve people. A Scottish fold needs company. Owners who work or go to school should think about getting a second cat. The cats will keep each other company during the day.

Other cats and toys are not enough, though. Owners must spend some time with their Scottish folds each day. A daily play session is enough exercise for this breed. Once the Scottish fold is tired out, it will be happy to curl up and take a nap. They usually curl up near their favorite person, too.

Scottish folds have quiet voices. These cats may meow softly to let their owners know when they want something. They also **communicate** by moving their ears. A cat listening to its owner will move its ears in the direction of his or her voice. Even when an owner does not speak, a Scottish fold will show interest by lifting up its ears.

A Scottish fold kitten may lose its ear fold when it is teething.

A Scottish fold is less likely to get into trouble if it has a friend to play with all day.

It is important to groom your cat each week, even if it helps groom itself.

Help Needed

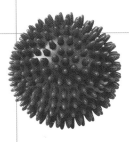

Owning a Scottish fold is a lot of fun. But it involves some work, too. Even if your cat has short hair, you will need to brush it once a week. Doing so will remove dirt and dead hair. Brushing also keeps the skin healthy. Longhaired cats should be combed twice a week.

Like most cats, Scottish folds are very clean. They **groom** themselves. But a Scottish fold may need a little help cleaning its ears. Cats with upright ears can usually wash their own ears. But Scottish folds with bent ears have a harder time. Cats with triple folds have the hardest time. Your **veterinarian** can show you how to clean your pet's ears.

It is important to take your Scottish fold to the veterinarian at least once a year. When healthy, this breed can live about 18 years. Keeping your pet healthy will help make sure your furry friend lives a long and happy life.

A longhaired Scottish fold is called a Highland fold.

Glossary

breed (BREED) A breed is a group of animals that are different from related members of its species. The Scottish fold is a popular cat breed.

cartilage (KAR-tuh-lij) Cartilage is an elastic tissue found throughout the body. Most Scottish folds' ears do not have cartilage.

communicate (kuh-MYOO-nuh-kate) To communicate is to pass information along. Scottish folds communicate by moving their ears.

gene (JEEN) A gene is the part of a cell that controls the appearance or growth of a living thing. A special gene produces the fold in Scottish folds' ears.

geneticist (juh-NET-it-cyst) A geneticist is a person who specializes in the way genes are passed on. A geneticist from the United States bought three kittens to study.

groom (GROOM) To groom is to clean and keep up the appearance. Scottish folds groom themselves.

misshapen (miss-SHAPE-uhn) To be misshapen is to have an ugly shape. Some Scottish folds can have misshapen heads if bred wrong.

tabby (TAB-ee) A tabby is a cat with a striped or spotted coat. Some Scottish folds have tabby coats.

upright (UHP-rite) To be upright is to be vertical. About one half of Scottish folds have upright ears.

veterinarian (vet-ur-uh-NER-ee-uhn) A veterinarian is a doctor who treats animals. It is important to take your cat to the veterinarian.

To Learn More

BOOKS

Bailey, Gwen. *What Is My Cat Thinking?* San Diego: Thunder Bay Press, 2010.

Gagne, Tammy. *Amazing Cat Facts and Trivia*. New York: Chartwell Books, Inc., 2011.

WEB SITES

Visit our Web site for links about Scottish fold cats:
www.childsworld.com/links

Note to Parents, Teachers, and Librarians: We routinely verify our Web links to make sure they are safe and active sites. So encourage your readers to check them out!

Index